CAN SCIENCE SOLVE?

THE MYSTERY OF
ESP

REVISED AND UPDATED

Chris Oxlade

Heinemann Library

Chicago, Illinois

Customer Service 888-454-2279

Visit our website at www.heinemannraintree.com

Editorial: Adam Miller, Catherine Veitch
Design: Philippa Jenkins
Production: Vicki Fitzgerald
Originated by Chroma Graphics (Overseas) Pte. Ltd
Printed and bound in China by Leo Paper Group
12 11 10 09 08
10 9 8 7 6 5 4 3 2 1

New edition ISBNs: 978-1-4329-1021-1 (hardcover)
                   978-1-4329-1027-3 (paperback)

Library of Congress Cataloging-in-Publication Data
Oxlade, Chris
  The mystery of ESP / Chris Oxlade.
    p. cm. -- (Can science solve?)
  Includes bibliographical references and index.
  Summary: Examines the phenomenon of ESP, or extrasensory perception,
  and the theories that exist to explain it.
  ISBN 1-58810-665-9
  1. Extrasensory perception--Juvenile literature. [1. Extrasensory perception.]
  I. Title: Mystery of extrasensory perception. II. Title. III Series.
  BF1321 .O85 2002
  113.8--dc21
                    2001004538

Acknowledgments
The author and publisher are grateful to the following for permission to reproduce copyright material: © BBC Natural History Unit/Peter Oxford: p24; © Corbis: p25; © Corbis/Bettman: p8–9; © Eye Ubiquitous: p6; © Fortean Pictures: pp12, 14, 17, 28; © iStockphoto/Nic Morley: p15; © Getty Images/ Charlie Schuck: p27; © Mary Evans Picture Library: pp7, 10, 23, 26; © Photolibrary/Ghislain & Marie De Lossy: p5; © Rex Features: p22; © Science Photo Library: p 4; © Stockbyte: pp11, 20.

Cover photograph © Alamy/PhotoAlto/Frederic Cirou.

The publishers would like to thank Charlotte Guillain for her assistance in the preparation of this book.

Some words are shown in bold, **like this**. You can find the definition for these words in the glossary.

CONTENTS

UNSOLVED MYSTERIES

For centuries, people have been puzzled and fascinated by mysterious places, creatures, and events. Is there really a monster living in Loch Ness? Did the lost city of Atlantis ever exist? Are UFOs tricks of the light, or actually vehicles from outer space? Do some people know what you are thinking through the power of extrasensory perception?

Some of these mysteries have baffled scientists, who have spent years trying to find the answers. But just how far can science go? Can it really explain the unexplained? Are there some mysteries that science simply cannot solve? Read on and make up your own mind . . .

This book tells you about the mystery of extrasensory perception (ESP). It explains what ESP is, gives some amazing examples of ESP, and tells you about the science of **parapsychology** and the experiments that scientists are doing to try to find out whether ESP really exists.

Nostradamus (1503–1566) was a French astrologer who predicted many modern events. Was it ESP or luck?

What is extrasensory perception?

How many times have you said to somebody, "I knew you were going to say that," or, "That's exactly what I was thinking"? Have you ever correctly guessed the result of a football game or which way up a coin will land several times in a row? Or have you dreamed about something happening and woken up to find out that it actually happened? If you have, then perhaps you have experienced extrasensory perception!

Extrasensory perception means being aware of something or knowing what somebody is thinking without using any of the normal five senses—sight, hearing, touch, smell, and taste. Sometimes ESP is called the "sixth sense."

ESP is an example of a **paranormal phenomenon**. "Paranormal" means anything that cannot be explained by normal science. Some people think that ESP simply is not possible. Other people believe that they have the power of ESP, or that other people have the power. Others are yet to be convinced. Is there anything science can do to solve this mystery?

How many times have your dreams come true?

BEGINNINGS OF A MYSTERY

Nobody knows when people first started to notice **paranormal** events such as extrasensory perception. For thousands of years, people all over the world have believed in gods or have had **superstitions**. Many people think that the mind and body are separate, and that souls live on after death. To them, many paranormal events, such as knowing about what will happen in the future, can be explained by their religious beliefs. Only since the development of modern science in the last few hundred years have people begun to investigate paranormal events in a serious way.

The spiritualist movement

The thing that first got scientists interested in paranormal events was the beginning of the **spiritualist** movement in the 19th century. Spiritualists believe that the spirits of dead people can communicate with living people. The spiritualist movement began in 1848 with a strange event. Two U.S. sisters, Katherine and Margaret Fox, heard peculiar knocking noises in their home. They could not find anything making the noises, so they decided that the sounds were being made by the spirit of a dead person trying to contact them.

Aboriginal people believe they can tell by ESP when a family member is harmed.

6

Spiritualists attempt to contact the spirits of the dead at meetings called **seances**. A person called a medium leads the seance. He or she is the connection between the living people at the meeting and the spirits they are trying to contact. Spirits are said to make themselves known by making noises, moving objects in the room, or speaking through the medium.

Early scientific investigations

One of the first scientific investigations into spiritualism was carried out in the 1880s by the UK scientist Sir William Crookes. The Society of Psychical Research was founded in England in 1882, and in the United States in 1885, to conduct scientific investigations into spiritualism and other paranormal **phenomena** that were popular at the time, such as fortune telling, ghostly hauntings, and **levitation**. The society is still going today.

In the 1930s, scientists at Duke University, in North Carolina, set up a laboratory to do scientific tests into the paranormal. In charge was the famous psychologist Joseph Banks Rhine, who invented the term "extrasensory perception." Among his experiments were some to test whether people really did have the power of ESP.

Joseph Banks Rhine and his wife worked together on ESP experiments.

DID YOU SENSE THAT?

Here are some examples of people who claimed to have sensed things by ESP. Have you had any similar experiences yourself?

Super powers?

The comic book writer John Byrne wrote a Spider-Man story in 2003 that involved an electrical blackout in New York. Six months later the city was hit by a real blackout. Another Spider-Man story involved an earthquake in Japan, and the real thing happened shortly afterward. Byrne also worked on a Superman comic book in which his hero flew to rescue a space shuttle that was in trouble. The Challenger space shuttle exploded very soon afterward. Byrne changed his story out of respect for the victims.

Ducks in the sand

ESP often happens in dreams. In the late 19th century, in Kent, England, a woman whose last name was Busk had a dream that she was walking in her father's farmyard when she saw the heads of several ducks sticking out of the ground! In the morning, a worker from the farm visited and said that there had been a strange robbery. The robbers had stolen some ducks, but left several of them buried in sand, with only their heads showing. Did Miss Busk somehow "see" the robbery by ESP?

Dreaming of a disaster

On the morning of October 20, 1966, nine-year-old Eryl Mai Jones woke up in the town of Aberfan, in Wales. She told her mother that she had had a nightmare. She had dreamed that she had gone to school in the morning but found "something black had come down all over it." The very next day, disaster struck. A massive heap of waste from the nearby coal mines slipped downhill like a mudslide, burying the local school. Sadly, 144 people were killed, including Eryl. Many other people in Aberfan also claimed to have dreamed that the disaster would happen.

Did some people predict the dreadful events in Aberfan?

ESP OR COINCIDENCE?

If a person has experienced ESP, what possible explanation could there be? There are really only three choices . . .

1 The person could be lying! For example, people could say they dreamed that an event was going to happen after it actually did. Nobody could say for sure that it was a lie. In many cases, we just have to trust that they really had the experience.

2 It could simply be a **coincidence**, rather than ESP. People could imagine an event before or at the same time as it actually happens, purely by chance. In the first example on page 8, there is a chance that the comic book writer was just lucky to think about a blackout and an earthquake in his storylines. You can read more about coincidence on the next page.

3 ESP really does exist. This can only be proved by doing careful experiments.

Some passengers canceled their voyages on the Titanic after they apparently dreamed of the disaster.

It is probably a coincidence . . .

Most people who experience events that seem to be caused by ESP think that ESP is at work, because the chances of the event happening by coincidence seem extremely small. For example, it seems highly unlikely that a person could be dreaming about ducks buried in the ground at the same time that ducks are actually found buried.

But most scientists argue that many events that seem to be caused by ESP can actually be explained by coincidence. This is because things that seem unlikely can actually be more likely than you would think. For example, if you were in a room with 21 other people, you might think it was an amazing coincidence if two people in the room shared the same birthday. In fact, the laws of probability (which are a way of calculating how likely something is to happen) say that the chance of this happening is about one in two, which is the same chance as a coin landing on heads.

Imagine that you dream about your friend slipping on a banana peel and find out the next day that he or she did so. Using the laws of probability, we can figure out that this sort of coincidence happens every couple of weeks.

Would it be coincidence, luck, or the work of ESP if you threw several double sixes?

THE SCIENCE OF PARAPSYCHOLOGY

Let's look at some of the words that scientists and other people who study paranormal phenomena use.

Psychology is the scientific study of the human mind and how people think and behave. **Parapsychology** is the branch of psychology that studies strange events that cannot be explained by other areas of science like physics, biology, and normal psychology. It is also known as psychical research. The word "psychical" is often shortened to "psi." A **psychic** is a person who regularly has paranormal experiences. Many scientists take paranormal events very seriously, and several universities around the world have departments of parapsychology that carry out research to find out if paranormal events really happen.

Parapsychologists divide ESP into three different areas. They are **telepathy**, **clairvoyance**, and **precognition**. Another area of the paranormal, called **telekinesis**, is closely linked to ESP.

Monica Nieto Tejada from Spain is apparently able to read words clairvoyantly that are in a sealed box. Here she appears to guess correctly the target word: "truth."

Telepathy

Telepathy is using ESP to sense what people are thinking, how they are feeling, or even what they know. For example, one person might telepathically sense that his or her friend is feeling unhappy. The distance between the two people does not matter—telepathy is said to work whether they are in the same room or on opposite sides of the world. People who claim to be able to sense thoughts or feelings by telepathy are described as telepathic. Telepathy is also known as mind reading.

Clairvoyance

Clairvoyance is sensing objects or events that are happening by ESP. For example, a person might sense by clairvoyance that an accident has happened. Like telepathy, clairvoyance is said to work over any distance. So a person who senses objects and events by clairvoyance, who is called a clairvoyant, can sense them whether they are next door or hundreds of miles away. Clairvoyants often "see" things happening in dreams or when they are in a trance.

Precognition

Precognition is using the powers of ESP to know what is going to happen in the future. For example, a person might dream that an accident is going to happen the next day. This would be an example of precognition by clairvoyance.

PARAPSYCHOLOGY EXPERIMENTS

Many people claim that they have the power of ESP. They might say that they always know what members of their family are thinking, or that they are very good at guessing which way up a coin will land, or that they always predict the results of football games correctly. They may be right, but their claims are not scientific proof that ESP exists.

The only way of finding out whether ESP really exists is by doing experiments. The idea of an ESP experiment is to test how successful a person is at guessing what symbols or numbers appear on a computer screen or on a series of cards that he or she cannot see. The person being tested is called the **receiver**. In **telepathy** experiments there is also another person who thinks of the images or numbers so that the receiver can detect another person's thoughts. This person is called the **sender**.

A pack of Zener cards contains cards with these five symbols.

Today, people can take computerized Zener card tests. Some exist on the Internet.

Simple ESP experiments

In modern experiments, **parapsychologists** nearly always use computers to choose the images or numbers that the receiver tries to sense by ESP. This is because a computer is likely to choose images or numbers more **randomly** than a human would. But until the 1970s, parapsychologists used sets of cards to choose instead. One of the best-known experiments was devised by Joseph Banks Rhine. Here is how it works.

The experiment uses a pack of cards called Zener cards. On one side of each card is a simple symbol—either a square, a circle, a cross, a star, or some wavy lines. A complete pack contains five cards of each symbol, making a total of 25 cards.

The cards are shuffled so that they are in completely random order, then they are placed face down in a pile. The person in charge of the test takes one card off the pile. The receiver (the person being tested), who cannot see the cards, writes down which of the five symbols he or she thinks the tester is holding. The tester writes down whether the receiver is right or wrong.

MORE EXPERIMENTS

A modern ESP experiment used by **parapsychologists** is called the Ganzfeld experiment. Parapsychologists at the Koestler **Parapsychology** Unit at the University of Edinburgh, in Scotland, have been running this experiment on people since the mid-1990s. The experiment has been designed so that the **receiver** is not distracted by sights or sounds, which means there is no chance of cheating.

How it works

The receiver lies down in a special room, called a sensory deprivation chamber. The room has thick walls that stop sound from getting in, and it is dark except for a dim red light. The receiver wears half a ping-pong ball over each eye and headphones through which a **random** hissing sound, called white noise, is played. These devices stop the receiver from using his or her normal senses and help the receiver to go into a dream-like state. This increases the chances of the receiver sensing by ESP. In a completely separate room, a computer picks random video clips from a huge library of different clips. A **sender** watches the video clips carefully. The receiver in the chamber describes what images he or she is thinking about or "receiving" from the sender. The descriptions are recorded on tape. When the test is finished, the receiver is played the recording he or she made for each video clip, together with four video clips, one of which is the one the sender saw. The other three were never seen by the sender. The receiver has to decide which of the clips is the correct one.

This woman is taking part in a Ganzfeld test.

Experiment results

To figure out what the results of parapsychology experiments mean, we have to understand some mathematics called probability. It is all about how likely it is for an event to happen. Imagine trying to guess the toss of a coin. The probability that you guess correctly is one in two, because you can either guess heads or tails. If you guessed right, you would probably think you were just lucky. If you did that same test 100 times, you would expect to guess right about 50 times. But if you guessed right 60 times or more, you might think you were guessing with the help of ESP.

In the experiment above, you would guess one in four video clips correctly by luck alone. If you got an average of, say, one or two clips right over a series of 1,000 tests, you might have powers of ESP.

TRY IT YOURSELF

Do you have the power of ESP? Or do any of your friends or family? You can find out by doing some simple ESP tests of your own. Try this experiment. It is a test for clairvoyance, because the receiver is trying to guess the symbols on hidden cards. For the test you need two people—a person to be tested (the receiver) and a person to be the tester, or sender, who runs the experiment. Here is how to test a friend or member of your family.

The Zener card experiment

You need:

- Cardboard
- Scissors
- A marker
- A sheet of paper
- A blindfold

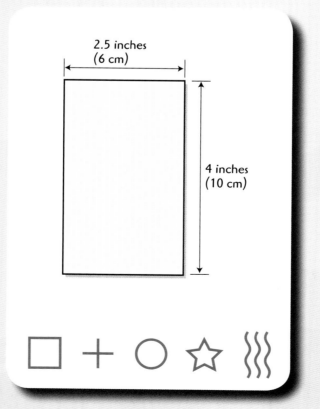

2.5 inches
(6 cm)

4 inches
(10 cm)

1 First, make a pack of Zener cards. Cut out 25 pieces of cardboard, each around 4 x 2.5 inches (10 x 6 cm). On five of the cards, draw a circle. On another five draw a square. On another five draw a cross. On another five draw a star. On the last five draw three wavy lines.

2 Draw the five symbols along the edge of a piece of paper, with a card-shaped box next to each one. The cards will be placed on this paper in five piles.

3 Ask the receiver to sit on one side of a table. Put a blindfold on him or her. You sit on the opposite side of the table. Collect the Zener cards into a pack. Shuffle them lots of times to make sure they are in **random** order, and place them face down on the table.

4 Ask the receiver to use his or her mind to try to "see" the symbol on the card on top of the pack. When the receiver has made a guess, put the card, still face down (and without looking at it), on the sheet of paper next to the symbol that the receiver said.

5 Now do same thing for the next card. Keep going until all the cards are used up. Now the receiver can take the blindfold off.

6 Pick up each of the piles of cards in turn, and count how many cards match the symbol the receiver chose. Write down this number. Add the numbers together to get the total number of cards that the receiver got right.

How did your receiver do? Just by chance, he or she should have gotten around five cards right. If he or she scored more, your receiver could have powers of ESP. If so, repeat the test. If the receiver keeps getting more than five, perhaps ESP does exist!

You could repeat the test with the tester actually looking at the cards and trying to "send" the image by thought. This would be a test for **telepathy**.

WHAT EXPERIMENTS TELL US

The results of some early ESP experiments, such as those carried out by Joseph Banks Rhine, seemed to show that ESP does exist. For example, in Zener card tests carried out in the 1930s, some people got more than five cards out of 25 correct in almost every test they took. One man named Adam Linzmayer had amazing results. The chances of him getting these results by luck were 1.7 billion to one. Some **parapsychologists** claim that results like these show beyond a doubt that ESP exists.

The recent results of some Ganzfeld experiments (see page 16) also seem to show that some people have powers of ESP. Some people have gotten results of 40 percent again and again. (Remember that the average results are one in four, or 25 percent.) In fact, these results show that the chances of ESP not existing are a million to one! However, most Ganzfeld tests have given no positive results.

Do you think you could guess what was on these cards? What would the results prove?

Skeptics versus believers

Many modern-day scientists are **skeptical** about positive results from ESP experiments. They claim that the early experiments were poorly designed, that cheating could have been easy, and that the experiments were not carried out scientifically. They also criticize modern experiments because the experiments can produce one result one day and a different result the next day, showing that their positive results were just luck. Skeptics also say that parapsychologists tend to ignore negative results that show that ESP does not exist and only keep positive results. The skeptical scientists call this "selective thinking."

Parapsychologists defend their results against the criticisms of skeptical scientists. They say that the scientists would never be satisfied with the results, because they are already convinced that ESP does not exist. They also say that the scientific methods we use today cannot show how ESP works, and that we should not worry about whether we think ESP is possible or not, but rather just accept the results.

If ESP does exist . . .

If parapsychologists prove that ESP does exist, how could it work? How exactly could a thought get from one person's mind to another's? Some parapsychologists say that people have some sort of "mind-field" around them that is projected from their brains. But the field is very weak, and it can only be detected if other senses are suppressed, as happens in the Ganzfeld experiment. There is no scientific evidence for such mind-fields.

MORE PARANORMAL EVENTS

Closely linked to telepathy, clairvoyance, and precognition (the three forms of ESP), and studied by the same parapsychologists, is another paranormal phenomenon called telekinesis or psychokinesis ("PK" for short). Telekinesis is the ability to affect objects by mind power alone, without touching them.

Spoon bending

Among the most spectacular demonstrations of the power of telekinesis has been spoon bending! The most famous spoon-bender in the world is Uri Geller. Geller can apparently take a perfectly ordinary metal spoon, hold it lightly in his fingers, and make it bend and eventually break in two. On many occasions, his demonstrations in a television studio have appeared to have had an effect on objects in the homes of the people watching the programs. There have even been reports of bent spoons found in kitchen drawers and of old watches re-starting!

Skeptical scientists have claimed that Geller uses trickery to perform his stunts. Many have tried to prove this.

Uri Geller poses with a spoon that was apparently bent by mind power alone.

Throwing dice

Parapsychologists have done experiments to see if telekinesis actually does exist. One of the simplest experiments tests whether a person can influence which way up dice land. The person calls the number he or she wants, then the die is thrown, normally by a machine to prevent the tester from influencing the results.

Results of this experiment have shown that some people do seem to have powers of telekinesis. However, the results are not so good when tests have been carried out in strict laboratory conditions. It may be that some testers help their **subjects** without knowing it.

You could try a similar experiment yourself. Think of a number on the die and try to make the die land that way up, using your mind. Throw the die 60 times. The die should land on your number around 10 times by luck. If you get more, perhaps you have the power of telekinesis.

Hovering in the air

Some people claim to be able to lift objects, including themselves, into the air by telekinesis. This is known as **levitation**. One of the most famous examples of levitation was the 19th-century British **psychic** Daniel Dunglas Home, who is said to have levitated himself regularly. Many reliable eyewitnesses confirmed that he did so.

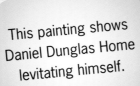

This painting shows Daniel Dunglas Home levitating himself.

ANIMALS WITH ESP

Humans are not the only creatures that seem to have powers of ESP. There are many tales of cats and dogs that seem to know by some sort of sixth sense when their owners are in trouble or are coming home from work. Other stories tell of how lost cats and dogs have found their way home, in some cases across whole continents! Other animals seem to be capable of amazing feats of **navigation**, or of sensing impending disasters, such as earthquakes, before they happen. Perhaps they have some extra senses that we do not understand yet, and that humans used to have hundreds of thousands of years ago. Here are some examples . . .

Go home, Maxl!

Researchers in Germany carried out an experiment on a sheepdog named Maxl. Maxl was driven nearly 4 miles (about 6 kilometers) from home to an area he did not know, then was released and watched. He found his way home after an hour and 18 minutes. When the experiment was repeated two weeks later, Maxl got home in just half the time.

Greater Shearwaters migrate to a tiny group of islands in the Atlantic Ocean. Nobody knows how they do it.

Animal supersenses

Many animals have senses that are far better than human senses, or have extra senses that humans do not have. For example, dogs can hear sounds with very high pitch, fish can sense movements in water with pressure sensors, and snakes can detect tiny changes in the temperature of objects around them. There is scientific evidence that **migrating** birds sense the angle of the Sun's rays and use them to navigate, even when it is cloudy. They can also detect Earth's **magnetic field** and may be able to read the pattern of stars so that they can fly at night.

Avoiding an avalanche

One morning in 1939, the St. Bernard dogs that belonged to a **monastery** in the Swiss Alps refused to go for their walk. They had never done this before. After several attempts, the dogs refused to budge, and so the monks gave up, mystified. That same morning, an avalanche wiped out the path that the monks and dogs would have taken.

Do you think the St. Bernard dogs, like this one, sensed an oncoming disaster?

FACT OR FICTION?

The most difficult thing about ESP and other paranormal phenomena is deciding what and whom to believe. In most cases, we only have the word of one person to go by. Many ESP events could be faked, some probably have been, and some definitely have been.

Mark Twain's dream

In writer Mark's Twain's autobiography, he claims that in 1858 he had a frightening dream in which he saw his brother Henry in a metal coffin with white and red flowers on his chest. Several weeks later, Henry was killed in an accident. When Twain saw the body, it was exactly as he had dreamed. This story appears in many books about the paranormal, but there is no record of Twain telling it at the time of his brother's death, and some friends of Twain said that most of his autobiography was "fiction."

Author Mark Twain claimed to have had a paranormal experience.

Magic tricks

Magicians often do tricks that make them appear to have the power of ESP. How many times have you seen a magician guess a card that has been selected at **random** by a member of the audience, or guess what picture a person has drawn? But these tricks are done by trickery rather than ESP.

Most magicians do not seriously claim to have powers of ESP, but are some people who claim to have ESP really just magicians? Some magicians are not very happy about this! The most famous is a magician named James Randi, who claims that all ESP and **telekinesis** events are magic tricks.

In 1979 two teenagers, Michael Edwards and Steve Shaw, asked for their **psychic** powers to be investigated by scientists at Washington University. After three years and many amazing feats of ESP and telekinesis that convinced the scientists, they admitted that they had done everything by trickery!

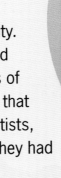

Is this woman really **levitating**? Does she have the power of telekinesis, or is it just a magic trick?

Why fake ESP?

Why do people want to try to trick others into thinking that they have the power of ESP? People are very interested in the paranormal, so individuals who could show they had paranormal powers like ESP would be really famous. They could make money by appearing on television and writing books. But some do it just for fun!

WHAT DO YOU THINK?

So, can science really solve the mystery of ESP? Some examples of ESP seem to show that something unusual is going on. But finding out for sure is proving to be difficult. Most scientists are yet to be persuaded that ESP exists, because there is no solid evidence.

Are the theories about the existence of ESP convincing?

- No experiments that seemed to show ESP exists have ever been repeated under laboratory conditions, which is the proof that is really needed.

- Many apparent examples of ESP have turned out to be hoaxes.

- Many stories of ESP are probably just **coincidence**.

BUT . .
- Many **parapsychologists** and millions of ordinary people believe that ESP does exist.

- Most scientists do not dismiss ESP completely, even though they may think it is unlikely.

Now that you have read about ESP and the scientific investigations into it, can you draw any conclusions?

- Did you try the experiments in this book?

- Did the results convince you either way?

- Do you have any theories of your own about how ESP works, or why it could never work?

- Do you believe the people who say they have had ESP experiences?

- Or do you believe the scientists who say that there is no proof at all?

Try to keep an open mind. Bear in mind that if scientists throughout history had not bothered to investigate everything that appeared to be strange or mysterious, many scientific discoveries may never have been made.

Can a fortune teller really predict the future through a crystal ball?

GLOSSARY

clairvoyance sensing the existence of objects or events by extrasensory perception

coincidence when two events happen at the same time, purely by chance

levitation lifting a person or object off the ground without touching him or her or using any machine

magnetic field region around a magnet where the magnet's effect can be felt. Earth behaves as though it has a huge magnet inside it and a magnetic field around it.

migrate move long distances from one part of the world to another at certain times of the year

monastery place where monks live, worship, and work

navigation finding the way from place to place

paranormal describes anything that cannot be explained by normal sciences like physics or biology

parapsychologist person who studies events that cannot be explained by other branches of science like physics or biology

parapsychology scientific study of events that cannot be explained by other branches of science like physics or biology

phenomenon strange or remarkable thing or event. The plural is phenomena.

precognition knowing what is going to happen in the future by extrasensory perception

psychic person who regularly has paranormal experiences

psychology study of the mind and how people think and behave

random without any sort of pattern. For example, a coin lands on head or tails randomly.

receiver person who is being tested in a telepathy experiment. The receiver tries to detect, or "receive," images or numbers by ESP.

seance meeting to communicate with spirits

sender person in telepathy experiments who thinks of images or numbers so that a "receiver" can try to detect his or her thoughts

skeptical critical or unbelieving. A person who is skeptical is called a skeptic.

spiritualist person who believes that we can communicate with the souls of people who have died

subject person on whom an experiment is carried out

superstition belief in something supernatural

telekinesis ability to make objects move by thought power alone

telepathy sensing what people are thinking by using extrasensory perception

Find out more

You can find out more about ESP in books and on the Internet. Use a search engine such as www.yahooligans.com to search for information. Try searching for words such as "extrasensory perception" or something more specific, such as "Ganzfeld experiments," to help you find what you are looking for.

More books to read

Harvey, Gill. *ESP*.
Tulsa, Okla.: EDC, 1999.

Herbst, Judith. *ESP*.
Minneapolis: Lerner, 2005.

Miller, Connie Colwell. *Psychics (Unexplained)*.
Mankato, Minn.: Capstone, 2007.

Websites

Take a Zener cards test at www.mdani.demon.co.uk/para/esp1.htm

INDEX